To Eden

Please enjoy it

Hun Pay it

forward

CBel

A MAN CALLED RAVEN

PICTURES BY GEORGE LITTLECHILD

STORY BY RICHARD VAN CAMP

CHILDREN'S BOOK PRESS
SAN FRANCISCO, CALIFORNIA

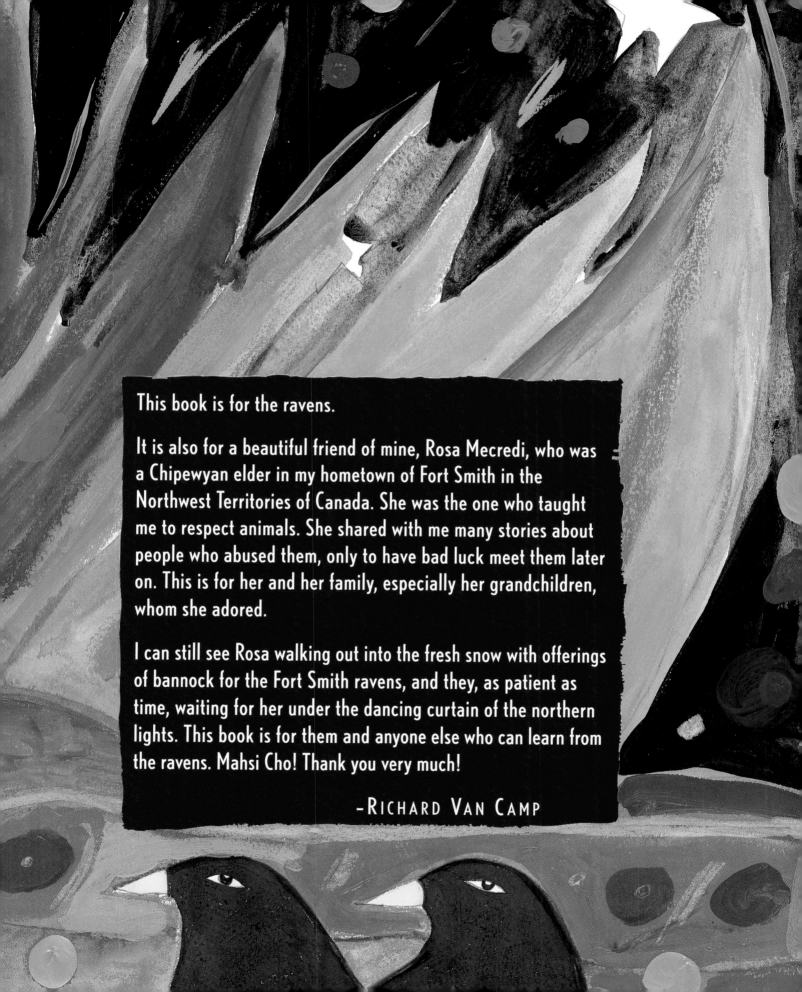

This book is for the ravens.

It is also for a beautiful friend of mine, Rosa Mecredi, who was a Chipewyan elder in my hometown of Fort Smith in the Northwest Territories of Canada. She was the one who taught me to respect animals. She shared with me many stories about people who abused them, only to have bad luck meet them later on. This is for her and her family, especially her grandchildren, whom she adored.

I can still see Rosa walking out into the fresh snow with offerings of bannock for the Fort Smith ravens, and they, as patient as time, waiting for her under the dancing curtain of the northern lights. This book is for them and anyone else who can learn from the ravens. Mahsi Cho! Thank you very much!

-RICHARD VAN CAMP

The two boys danced around madly, trying to corner the raven. They shouted at each other not to let it get away. The raven gave off metal screeches and hissed at them.

The boys had been hitting the bird with broken hockey sticks and now its wing was dragging. It half skipped, half waddled behind a pile of boxes stashed in their neighbor's garage.

Chris squinted. "Where is it? Where'd it go?"

Toby answered, "Dunno. It's gotta be in that corner somewhere. Go find it!" There was a big pause.

"I'm not going to find it. Forget that. You go find it!"

"No, sir. You first!"

The raven used this moment of confusion to roar its way between the two boys and out into the driveway. Feeling the thunder of wings, the boys yelled and grabbed each other. They spun around and the raven was gone.

Standing in front of them, however, was a huge man. And he was angry. "You kids!" he boomed. "What were you doing to that raven?"

Chris started to edge away, pulling his brother by the shirt, but the man blocked them. "We were trying to help it fly," Toby said. "It was hurt, and..."

"Silence!" the man roared. "You lie. Do you know what you have done? Can't you see what a great crime you have committed?"

"Hey, man," Chris started. "Take it easy. It was just a raven. Those things get into our garbage and spread it all over the street."

"Enough!" the man said. "Who are your parents?"

The boys winced. They knew they were in big trouble. The man towered above them. They knew they could not lie to him. He motioned for them to come forward, out into the sunlight.

It was Toby who finally answered. "Our folks are Gwen and Ken Greyeyes. We live three doors down."

"Bring me to them," the man said. And they led the stranger to their house.

They walked in and called out for their mom to come downstairs. They ran up to their room, passing their mom on the way. She had soapsuds on her hands and she asked who it was, but they did not answer. They hit their bunk beds and hoped there wouldn't be any spankings.

After a while, there was a knock on the door, but the boys pretended to be asleep. "Get up, you two!" their mom called, "I know you're awake." She told them to come downstairs. They were in deep trouble, she said, and she was very disappointed with them.

Toby and Chris walked downstairs with heads low and knees weak.

The man was waiting for them.

"**S**it down," their mother said. "I want you to listen to this man." She walked off into the kitchen, to where their father sat, and they did not talk but listened also to what the stranger had to say.

He sat across from the two boys, smoking some tobacco and sipping on coffee. The boys looked at each other. Smoking wasn't allowed in their house.

There was a long silence as the man looked at them. The boys noticed that he had long black hair and huge eyes. He wore old clothes and smelled of pine needles. Chris thought that there was probably nothing this man didn't see, and Toby wondered if the man ever slept.

The man took a long drag on his smoke and began to speak. "You don't know this, but you were asking for a lot of trouble when you were beating on that raven. Your parents told me that you have never gone out on the land. Well, maybe that explains your actions. But I want to tell you a story about a man who liked to hurt ravens. This is a true story, so listen and take from this what you can."

"In my day, there was this man. He was old and he was wicked. He never smiled and he never said anything nice to anyone." The man paused to take another drag on his smoke and a sip of his coffee.

Then he said, "Well, he used to shoot arrows at ravens. And one day he hit one of them. Now, he wasn't trying to kill them to eat them, he was trying to hurt them. He wasn't using the normal arrowheads. He was using blunts—and boys, you better believe that hurts."

"**T**hat raven couldn't fly and it couldn't do anything else either. So it started to follow the old man. Day and night it followed him. The man couldn't run to his friends because he didn't have any, and the raven just followed him wherever he went.

Pretty soon he couldn't sleep because he knew the raven was watching him. So one day the man started to get funny in the head, and he climbed a tree to sleep. The raven just sat and waited for him on the ground. Well, the man slept for a little while, but when he woke up the raven was still there."

"**A**fter that, the man walked day and night and only stopped once in a while to sleep up in a tree. Soon he started jumping from treetop to treetop just so he wouldn't have to see the raven. And one day when he was jumping, he slipped and fell. But when he fell, he never hit the ground. When he fell, he started to change. And do you know what he turned into?"

"A raven!" answered the boys.

"That's right," the man said. "But you know what?"

"What?" the boys asked.

"He was still just as mean as he had always been."

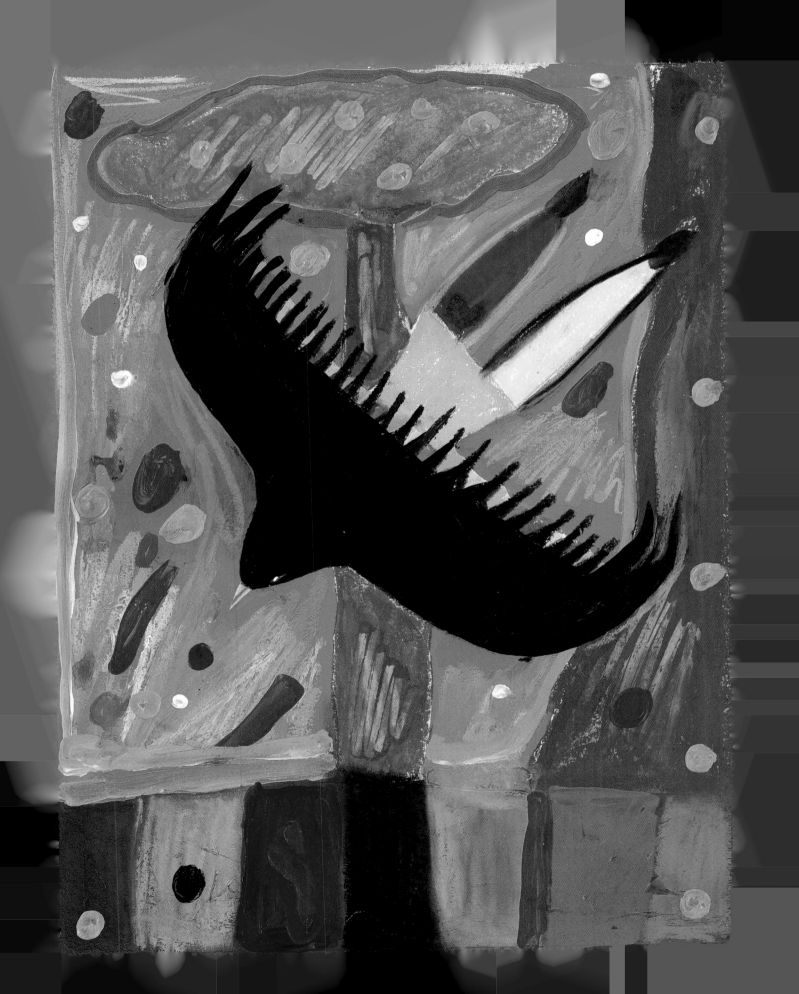

"That old man who became a raven flew back home so he could spy on all the people he used to know. He flew to his village, and when he got there he saw that there was a funeral. Do you know whose funeral that was?"

"The old man's."

"Yes. And do you know who came to the funeral?"

"No one," the boys said.

"Wrong," the man answered. "Everyone."

"What?" said Toby.

Chris said, "But I thought he... I thought you said... I thought nobody cared about him!"

"Yes," the man continued. "That's what the old man thought too. That's why he was so mean to everyone and that's why he liked to hurt ravens. But when he saw all the people singing for him, he knew he had a place in the village like everyone else. He knew he wasn't alone. Then he wanted to tell his people he was sorry, but he couldn't speak. He could only call out like the other ravens."

"**A**nd that was when the man who became a raven really started to change. That was when he started to watch over his people."

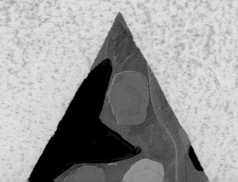

"He watched over his people when they went to the lakes to hunt moose...

and when they set nets to catch the fish coming down the river."

"He watched over his people as they hunted above the tree line for caribou. Once, there was an awful snowstorm, a whiteout, and his people got separated from each other. One group made shelters and was safe, but the other group started to walk in circles. He called out to the people lost in the snowdrifts, and they started to follow him. They followed him to the other group and they were saved. Raven saved them from freezing."

"**W**ow!" said Chris.

"That's amazing," said Toby.

"Yes," the man said. "And now do you see why you must respect Raven?"

"Yes," the boys answered. Their faces burned as they remembered what they had done.

"Well," the man said, "I think you've got the point. I had better go."

He put his coffee cup down and stood up. Chris and Toby followed him to the door. They wanted him to stay and tell them more stories about the animals and being an Indian.

"Mister," said Toby, "did that man ever get to become human again?"

The man paused before going out the door. "Sometimes, when there was something the people were forgetting, he would change back, but not for too long."

"Oh," they said, looking at each other.

Then the man was gone, leaving behind him the thunder of wings.

A MAN CALLED RAVEN is a contemporary story about a powerful and mysterious elder who teaches two young Indian brothers about respect for life. The elder tells the boys a story about an old man who hurt ravens and was transformed into a raven as punishment. Every once in a while, this raven becomes a man again to teach people that if you hurt any living thing you also hurt yourself–because all life is sacred and connected.

This book is an inspired collaboration between George Littlechild, an internationally acclaimed artist from the Plains Cree Nation of Canada, and Richard Van Camp, a young author from the Dogrib Nation of Canada's Northwest Territories. Although the cultures of these two Nations are very different, Littlechild was so moved by Van Camp's story that he agreed to create his own visual interpretation.

The story takes place in the Northwest Territories, where the northern lights dance, in the traditional lands of the Dogrib and Chipewyan Peoples who are part of the larger Dene nation. As Van Camp describes his home: "It's the jewel of Canada. Starting at the 60th parallel and heading north, that's where paradise is. Come visit!"

RICHARD VAN CAMP, the eldest of four boys, is a member of the Dogrib Nation from the Northwest Territories, Canada. He is a graduate of the University of Victoria and the En'owkin International School of Writing. He has published a novel, *The Lesser Blessed*, and his stories have been featured in many publications, including *Blue Dawn, Red Earth*, an anthology of Native American storytellers. His brothers are Rogey, Johnny, and Jamie!

GEORGE LITTLECHILD is an internationally renowned artist from the Plains Cree Nation. His first book for Children's Book Press, *This Land Is My Land* (1993), was the winner of both the prestigious Jane Addams Picture Book Award and the National Parenting Publications Gold Medal. In a starred review, *Publishers Weekly* called the book "a stunning gallery of art by a Native American of singular vision." Littlechild lives in Vancouver, British Columbia.

I dedicate this book to the following four people who inspired the characters in *A Man Called Raven*: John Powell who became the Raven Man; Marianne Sundown who became the mother; my nephew Jordan Smith who is the light haired boy; and another Jordan Smith (Marianne's son) who is the dark haired boy. Thank you to all. –G.L.

Story copyright© 1997 by Richard Van Camp. All rights reserved.
Pictures copyright© 1997 by George Littlechild. All rights reserved.
Editors: Harriet Rohmer and David Schecter
Consulting Editor: Alice Klein
Design and Production: John Miller, Big Fish
Editorial/Production Assistant: Laura Atkins

Thanks to Cliff Trafzer for his inspiration and support. And thanks to the staff of Children's Book Press: Andrea Durham, Janet Levin, Emily Romero, Stephanie Sloan, and Christina Tarango.

Children's Book Press is a nonprofit publisher of multicultural literature for children, supported in part by grants from the California Arts Council. Write us for a complimentary catalog: Children's Book Press, 246 First Street, Suite 101, San Francisco, CA 94105.

Library of Congress Cataloging-in-Publication Data
Van Camp, Richard
A man called raven/story by Richard Van Camp: pictures by George Littlechild. p. cm.
Summary: a mysterious man tells two Indian brothers why they must not hurt the ravens that pester them. ISBN 0-89239-144-8 (hardcover)
1. Metis-Juvenile fiction. [1. Metis-Fiction. 2. Indians of North America-Fiction. 3. Ravens-Fiction.] I. Littlechild, George, ill. II. Title
PZ7.V2725Man 1997 [Fic]-dc20 96-31905 CIP AC

Printed in Hong Kong through Marwin Productions
10 9 8 7 6 5 4 3 2 1